The

Brave

Whale

Also by Alan Temperley

Harry and the Wrinklies
Ragboy
Huntress of the Sea
The Simple Giant

ALAN TEMPERLEY

The Brave Whale

Illustrated by Nick Maland

This edition produced for the Book People Ltd,
Hall Wood Avenue, Haydock, St Helens WA11 9UL

First published in the UK by Scholastic Ltd, 1999
This edition published by Scholastic Ltd, 2005

Text copyright © Alan Temperley, 1999
Illustrations copyright © Nick Maland, 1999

ISBN 0 439 95486 X

Printed and bound by Nørhaven Paperback A/S, Denmark

The right of Alan Temperley and Nick Maland to be identified
as the author and illustrator respectively of this work has been asserted by
them in accordance with the Copyright, Designs and Patents Act, 1988.

CONTENTS

The Kidnapped Moon

For Liz and Ted

1

The Kidnapped Moon

Waldo Leander Fluke was a whale. He was young, with bright eyes, a nice grey skin, and a tail that was wider than the biggest stretch of your arms.

Although he was happy, Waldo was very shy. When the other young whales invited him to play, he swam away and hid.

Waldo had one close friend. This was the Moon. Every night he waited on the eastern horizon until it was time for her to come out and play.

"Hello, Waldo! I see you!" With bright hair and a dazzling smile she popped up into the sky.

Then they played games all over the oceans.

Sometimes, when the laughing Moon was low, Waldo jumped right over her back.

When the Moon was high, the young whale splashed in her silver waves and blew fountains into the air. The water sparkled like stars.

Late at night, when it was time for bed, Waldo carried the Moon far away to the western seas. Resting on his shoulders, she closed her eyes and slept.

But sometimes the wind blew loud and the weather was too rough for the Moon to come out and play. Then battling clouds covered the sky and the Moon hid away.

Waldo hid away too. The crashing waves frightened him.

Some creatures liked the black nights. These were the fierce, ragged-toothed, spiky, squirmy, stinging things that lived in the depths of the sea. Their leader, and King of the Underwater, was a giant octopus called Black Gogg.

In the pitchy dark they crept out of their caves and cracks in the weedy rocks. They were very wicked.

Black Gogg and his followers liked to tease Waldo. Although he was bigger, the young whale was afraid of them.

"Go on, give him a nip!" Black Gogg urged them. "This whale's nothing but a great baby! He's a coward!" And he puffed a cloud of ink into Waldo's eyes.

Black Gogg hated the Moon because she spread beautiful light all over the world. He liked the darkness; light made him shiver.

One day Black Gogg worked out a plan.

After the Sun had gone to bed and before the Moon rose, he sent a gang of spiky fish and eels and lobsters to chase Waldo far away.

Then Black Gogg and three giant squid – all red with sticky tentacles – swam off and hid under the waves at the eastern end of the sea. "Sssshhh!" whispered Black Gogg. With big saucer eyes he kept watch.

Soon the Moon came peeping over the horizon. She was a new moon, just a thin sickle of light, like a shell sitting on the sea.

"Waldo," she called happily. "Where are you?" This way and that she peered across the silvery water. "Waldo, are you coming out to play?"

Suddenly Black Gogg jumped out of the water and caught the Moon in his long tentacles. What a fright she got!

The green-eyed octopus was followed by his red companions, all shouting and splashing the water into foam.

"Games!" they cried roughly. "You've finished with games! No more games for you! Ha-ha! You're coming with us!"

Bravely the Moon struggled. Being so new and thin she was not very strong. The tentacles wrapped all around her and dragged her down, down, down, under the water.

Black Gogg and his squid tied up the poor Moon in a fishing net. Laughing with delight they swam off, dragging her behind.

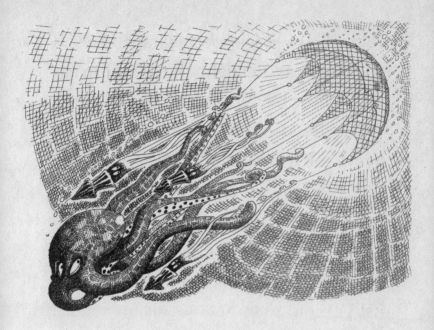

Deeper they went – and deeper. Gradually the Moon's light faded, fainter and fainter, shimmering into the depths. At length she was gone.

All over the world the night turned black.

Waldo could not see what was happening because the underwater gang had chased him into a bay with high cliffs. When the lookout, with eyes on stalks, saw the Moon's light vanish, he shouted to the others. At once they left Waldo alone and swam off to celebrate.

The young whale was very frightened. As soon as he had recovered, he left the bay and went looking for his friend. She was nowhere to be seen. He waited and waited. The sky remained black and Moonless.

Wondering what was wrong, Waldo swam to the east to meet her. Still the Moon did not appear. Waldo was very anxious.

"Have you seen my friend, the Moon?" he called to the stars.

"No, no! We can't help you," chirruped the stars, and flew off across the sky like a flock of sparrows. "We know nothing."

"Have you seen my friend, the Moon?" Waldo called to the lookout on a passing ship.

"No, I haven't seen her all night," answered the sailor. "It's very dark. I hope you find her soon."

"Have you seen my friend, the Moon?" the young whale called to a passing albatross.

"No-o-o," squawked the big bird, circling overhead. "Without her I've lost my wa-a-ay. Can you tell me how to reach the equa-a-tor?"

Waldo pointed.

"Tha-a-ank you." The albatross

chattered its beak and flew on.

Dawn came and the world filled with golden light.

"Have you seen my sister, the Moon?" the Sun called down to Waldo. "I was asleep. Now I am told that she is missing."

"I'm sorry," said Waldo. "I've been searching for her all night."

All over the world, from the snows of the South Pole to the jungles of Africa, there was consternation.

"Where is the Moon?" demanded the President of the United States of America.

"Where is the Moon?" said the astronaut, high up in his spaceship.

"Where is the Moon?" cried the

pygmy as he jumped from the jaws of a crocodile.

And all over the world, on land as well as in the sea, the secret, creepy things that hate light came crawling and wriggling and hopping out of marshes and deep caves. Good people barred their doors and windows and did not go out after sunset.

Waldo sang his song through all the oceans of the world. "Have you seen my friend? Have you seen my friend, the Moon?" But no one could help him.

At length Waldo came to the land of the Whisper Witch, who hears everything. She lived in a big cave on a lonely headland. Her hair was like mist, her fingers like seaweed, and her eyes were as clear as jellyfish.

"Have you seen my friend, the Moon?" Waldo asked nervously.

"No." The Witch's voice was faint as the scratch of a claw. "I have not seen her. But my whisperers have told me: the wild waves know; the pebbles know; the sea winds have breathed it into my ear. Black Gogg has stolen her – down, down, into the depths of the sea."

Her cloak of feathers hung in rags. "You must be brave, little whale. Only you can dive deep enough to save her."

Waldo turned and swam away. The words of the Whisper Witch frightened him very much. How could *he* rescue his friend from the kingdom of Black Gogg? Unhappily he blew a little spout into the air.

At sunset a sea-serpent swam past. Its mouth was full of teeth and coloured daggers stood up on its back.

"Are you still looking for the Moon?" it sniggered. "I wonder where she can be? Hee-hee-hee!"

Waldo rested in a sandy bay. For a long time he thought. He was too frightened to swim deep down to the kingdom of Black Gogg. He was a coward! Everyone said so.

But the thought of his friend, the happy Moon, being pulled down into the sea made Waldo angry. Frightened or not, he decided, he must swim a little way down to see what he could discover.

And so, in the middle of the night, when a few trembling stars showed between the clouds, the young whale swam to the middle of the ocean, right above Black Gogg's stronghold. Crossing his flippers for luck, he took several deep breaths – and dived.

Down he went – down and down and down. All was pitchy black.

At length, when Waldo thought he must soon be coming out at the other side of the world, he saw dim lights shining a long way ahead. Very quietly he swam closer.

In a wide, wild valley at the bottom of the sea, all the creatures of Gogg's kingdom were having a party. Eerie green light was provided by luminous fish that hung from the rocky walls and floated overhead. The sandy ground was covered with shipwrecks and skulls and jewels. A big stone table was spread with a feast. On a throne at the head of the table sat Black Gogg. A garland of weed and bones, shells and sharks' teeth was round his head and he was drinking rum from a golden goblet.

Quite close to the table a mountain of weed and seashells had been heaped up

on the valley floor. Around this a gang of
Gogg's followers was dancing excitedly:
they were all very spiky and squirmy and
stingy-looking. Lively music was
provided by a band of fiddler crabs.

A big catfish with rubbery whiskers
alighted on top of the mound.
Standing on his tail, he waved
his fins for silence.

When everyone was quiet he cleared his throat – "Ahem!" – and sang a song.

The shiny Moon came out to play,
Turned the midnight into day;
Gogg our leader, Gogg the brave,
Pulled her under the salty wave:
Bubble, bubble, miaow!

Now she sheds no silver light
Earth and sea are blackest night,
Rocky cave and weed and shell
Hide her beams extremely well:
Bubble, bubble, miaow!

When the catfish had finished, everyone cheered. Faster and faster, wilder and wilder, they pranced and whirled around Black Gogg and the pile of shells.

The crabs took up their fiddles for a new tune. All the party-goers joined fins and claws. Two by two they danced up and down, singing as they went:

The Moon is in the cave,
The Moon is in the cave,
    Blip, bloop and squirmio,
The Moon is in the cave.

Black Gogg waved a tentacle in time to the music.

When Waldo realized that his bright friend was buried underneath that giant heap of seaweed and shells he was very upset. He could not bear to see those horrid creatures dancing and laughing at her. It made him angry. She would *have* to be rescued.

And before he knew what he was doing, Waldo Leander Fluke, the timid young whale, gave a swish with his great tail and dived headlong into the middle of the party.

What a fright they got! The dwellers in the deep sea were flabbergasted. Some laughed and pointed – but not for long. They did not laugh as Waldo swam at them, bumping them aside with his great head, chasing them with his white teeth, bashing them with his flippers and strong tail.

The party came to a sudden end. Like

most bullies, the followers of Black Gogg were cowards at heart. When Waldo was frightened, they had teased him and nipped him. Now he dived at them, they scattered with cries of alarm and hid away in weedy hollows and cracks in the rocks.

Soon only Black Gogg himself was left – Black Gogg, the giant octopus and King of all the Underwater. With eyes as round as cartwheels and green as gooseberries, he watched the fierce young whale and waved threatening arms.

"If I catch you, young Waldo Fluke," he warned in a terrible voice, "we'll have you on this table for dinner! So swim away, while you still have a chance!"

Waldo did not listen. Instead, he threw the table upside down. Then he lashed his tail and swam straight at Black Gogg. There was a tremendous THUMP. Head over heels Black Gogg and his crusty throne went tumbling across the sea bed.

Cautiously, Black Gogg untangled his tentacles. Although he was big and strong and a bully, at heart he was the biggest coward of them all. When he saw how brave the young whale had become, he did not dare to fight him. Instead, he blew out a cloud of ink and disappeared.

When the water had cleared, Black Gogg was nowhere to be seen. The bony, jewel-scattered valley was deserted. Though if Waldo had looked *very* hard, he might just have seen the shivering tip of one black tentacle and gleam of saucer eyes peeping from a shipwreck.

Waldo gazed at the mountain of shells and seaweed that covered his friend, the captive Moon. Was she safe, he wondered. Was she hurt? Carefully he bulldozed the mound with his big head and fanned it away with his tail. A storm of sand and pebbles and seaweed filled the valley.

At length chinks of light began to appear through the whirling shells. Waldo worked on. Soon he had uncovered the mouth of a big cave. It was dazzling.

The young whale swam into the light.

"Oh, Waldo!" The Moon's eyes were full of tears. "I've been so unhappy! I thought no one would ever come."

She was still imprisoned in the net. A ring of big stones trapped her in the middle of the cave.

"I'll soon have you free." Waldo tore a hole in the net with his sharp teeth.

Gently he helped the Moon from the

cave. When Black Gogg caught her she had been a new Moon, thin as a smile. Now she had grown full and was as round as an orange. As she floated out into the valley, her beams lit every corner of Gogg's horrid kingdom. All the deep-sea citizens hid away in the blackest shadows of their holes.

Waldo took the Moon on his shoulders. "Hold on tight," he said, and carried her up – up – up – up to the splashing surface of the sea.

With a shout of joy the Moon sprang from his back and sailed high up into the heavens.

Waldo was pleased to get to the surface as well; he had nearly run out of breath.

*

All over the world people saw the Moon laughing in the sky. Everybody shouted and pointed and was glad – sailors and camel-drivers, policemen and children. The animals were glad too – tigers and fieldmice, polar bears and elephants.

But burglars and bandits did not like the Moon's light. "Grrr!" they growled and shook their fists. And all the wicked creatures hurried back into their caves and marshes.

Out in the bright ocean, all the whales and flying fish and seabirds came racing to congratulate Waldo. They made him a hero. Water splashed high as they leaped and dived in celebration.

*

And Waldo Leander Fluke, the shy young whale, was never frightened again – not of Black Gogg, or storms, or anything.

And his best friend of all, the big bright Moon, shone happily down on their games.

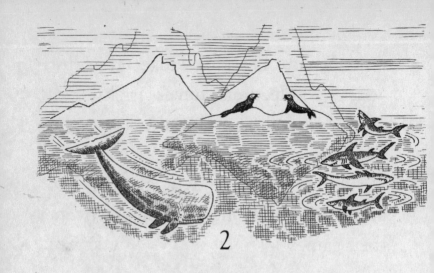

2

Waldo's Arctic Adventure

It was magic beneath the iceberg, every blue in the world. Waldo Leander Fluke, the adventurous young whale, gazed about him.

A shoal of sharks circled in the distance. Their teeth were like saws and they kept peeping out of the water.

Waldo lashed his tail and swam at them fiercely.

At once the sharks scattered and vanished into the ocean.

Waldo laughed and jumped into the air in a fountain of icy drops.

It was very cold but Waldo stayed warm inside his thick grey skin.

The iceberg rose above him like a fairy castle. Fat seals lay on silvery ledges. Seabirds flew overhead. Lines of geese, like scribbles, crossed the bright arctic sky.

To Waldo's surprise a thin trail of smoke rose into the air.

In front of a little cave in the iceberg an Eskimo boy was smoking fish. His black hair hung in a fringe. His trousers and jacket were edged with fur.

When he saw Waldo, the boy picked

up a spear to defend himself. Waldo saw that he walked with a limp.

"Don't hurt me," Waldo said. "I want to be your friend. What are you doing here? What's wrong with your leg? What are you burning on an iceberg?"

The Eskimo boy laid aside his spear and came to the water's edge. His name was Zadook. He looked very small beside the friendly whale.

"I went hunting from the village," he said. "In my kayak. Then the frost-smoke came and I got lost.

"When the frost-smoke went away," said Zadook, "I was out of sight of land. So I paddled to this iceberg. I was going to climb it and look from the top. But a big shark caught my kayak in his teeth. He hurt my leg. I was lucky he didn't eat me up." Fearfully he looked down into the water.

"It's safe now," Waldo said. "I chased the sharks away."

"I hate sharks." The Eskimo boy shivered.

"They have to eat," Waldo said reasonably.

"But not me!" said Zadook.

"Then I climbed on to the ice and made my home in this cave," Zadook continued. "I caught some fish with my line and smoked them by burning the broken kayak." He pointed to a small stack of fish in the cave entrance.

"How will you get home again?" asked Waldo.

"I don't know." Zadook blinked hard. "My father and the people from the village will have been searching for me. By now they'll think I have drowned."

"I can take you home," said Waldo, "if you're brave enough and your leg isn't too sore. Tie that piece of rope in a big loop."

Zadook did so. Waldo took the rope in his mouth like a horse's reins.

"Now, climb on my shoulders," he said.

Nervously the Eskimo boy stepped from the ice. Waldo's grey back was as wide as a carpet.

"Hold on tight," he said.

The bright waves and sparkling foam swished along Waldo's side as they sped through the arctic sea. Zadook's hood blew back and his black hair streamed in the wind.

Clouds of seabirds wheeled overhead. Seals and dolphins leaped on every side.

"Whee! This is fantastic!" Zadook clapped Waldo's shoulder with a brown hand.

After a long time a range of white hills appeared ahead. Smoke rose from the huts and igloos of a small village that stood near the shore.

The seals and dolphins waved to Zadook and turned back to sea. The Eskimos hunted for a living!

When they saw the big whale swimming close, the Eskimos ran for

their kayaks and hunting spears.

"What is that on the whale's head?" cried an old grandfather.

A little girl shaded her eyes. "It's Zadook!" she cried.

"Zadook!" All the village raced to the water's edge. "Zadook's come back! Zadook!"

Zadook waved and shouted in a clear ringing voice:

"This is Waldo the whale! He rescued me from an iceberg, far out at sea. He's my friend."

Waldo stopped beside a broad shelf of ice. Zadook jumped ashore and ran to his mother and father. His sore leg left red footprints in the snow.

"Waldo saved my life!" he cried. "We must never hurt him."

For three days Waldo stayed near to the Eskimo village. All the boys and girls went for rides on his back.

When he grew hungry, he dived to the bottom of the sea and hunted for food.

Everyone was happy. They made a feast close to the shore. The women cooked giant fishcakes. Waldo took them gently from their fingers as they stood on the rocks.

But soon Waldo tired of the fuss. He did not like so many people. He was a wild whale, not a pet. Besides, there were many things to see in the Land of the Midnight Sun and soon it would be winter.

"Goodbye." Zadook flung his arms round his friend's neck.

"I'll come back to see you," Waldo promised. "On my way south."

"I bet you'll have lots of adventures," Zadook said.

Waldo blew a spout high above the Eskimos' heads. The drops of water froze in the bitter air.

For a month Waldo wandered the northern seas. All about him were the wonders of the arctic.

Frost-smoke, like wispy fairies, danced above the water.

All day long the sun, fat and golden, skimmed the ocean and shot searchlights high into the blue.

Icebergs like magic castles floated far and near.

Giant sea-creatures with long necks and spiky backs swam like ships along the horizon.

Russian and American submarines, secret as night, patrolled the depths of the sea.

And when the sun had set, the northern lights danced like coloured flames across the sky.

Sometimes the clean, clear sky vanished behind a purple cloak of storm clouds. Then snow blew from the North Pole, blinding, pattering, filling the air with spinning flakes.

And hiding in the blizzard came the snow ghosts – whirling, shifting, screaming shapes with tattered mouths and eyes like holes, that chased the young whale far across the sea.

"Whooo! Whissshhh!" they cried. "Ooooowwwww!" and stretched out long grey arms to catch him by the tail.

Waldo dived to escape, but when he surfaced there they were again, waiting to pounce, rushing across the water like nightmares.

He was glad when the blizzard stopped and the snow ghosts went away.

*

The days grew shorter.

One morning as he surfaced, Waldo was surprised to find the sea turning to a sort of soupy slush.

Goodness! he thought. If this is ice forming I'd better head south – and quickly.

Soon he found clear water, green as glass. But the frost-smoke had returned. It was terribly cold.

And an hour later, he found himself back among the slush.

"Hmm!" Waldo looked to his left. "Perhaps it's better this way."

He returned to clear water and swam to the east ... then the west ... then north again ... and south.

Lifting his head into the air, he looked around with bright eyes. On every side, right to the horizon, the silvery slushy sea spread out around him.

"Well, here's a fix!" the young whale said aloud. "What do we do now, Waldo?"

Hour by hour the soupy slush grew thicker – and harder. Suddenly it was slush no more – it was ice.

Waldo was trapped in a circle of sea a mile across.

Then he saw that inch by inch the ring of open water was getting smaller. As the little waves splashed up on to the ice, they froze.

Waldo was alarmed. Although he could stay under water for a whole hour, he had to come up to breathe. And if all the sea turned to ice…!

"Oh, Waldo!" he said again, and

jumped high to see above the frost-smoke.

Icebergs, jagged as mountains, rose above the dazzling sea. On every side, right to the horizon, the whole world was white and beautiful and frozen.

For three days and three nights Waldo swam from side to side, and round and round, and all the time his pool grew smaller.

He was very lonely.

Clouds blotted out the northern lights and it began to snow again. A blizzard, thick as feathers, closed the world to a tiny circle of sea.

"Wheee! Whooo!" Snow ghosts rushed out of the blackness.

Waldo gave a shout and dived quickly.

With dawn the blizzard ceased. The frosty, fiery sun crept above the icebergs and the world sparkled.

A polar bear with her cub came padding by.

"Hunters!" she called to Waldo. "Trappers and whalers!"

Waldo raised his head. A group of figures, tiny as ants on the snowfield, headed towards them.

"I'd dive deep and swim away if I was you," said the polar bear.

"I can't," said Waldo.

The cub wanted to play. He dipped a paw in the water and splashed Waldo's nose.

"Come along," called his mother briskly. "No time to dawdle. Best paw forward. Turn your toes in nicely like your daddy."

"Bye-bye," said the cub.

Waldo watched them go, then turned to face the approaching hunters.

The Eskimos carried harpoons and ropes and kayaks. Waldo did not like the look of them and swam to a safe distance.

A boy was with the hunters. A spear was in his hand and a coil of thick fishing line hung from his shoulder. He limped to the edge of the ice and stared hard.

"Look! It's the whale who saved my life!" He waved. "Waldo, it's me, Zadook!"

Waldo nodded and kept his distance.

The Eskimos dropped their traps and clustered beside the open water.

"Don't be frightened," said Zadook's father. Like his son, he had a black fringe and wore a jacket edged with fur. "We won't hurt you."

Waldo swam close. Zadook rubbed his big head.

"I'm trapped," Waldo said. "The ice is closing in."

Zadook's father looked worried. "Soon the whole sea will be frozen solid. What are you going to do?"

"I don't know." Waldo blew a little spout.

"We can stop the sea from freezing," said Zadook. "We can use hammers and pickaxes."

"But not for the whole winter," said his father. "Not in the blizzards. Not when it's dark all day. Not when the ice is two metres thick."

"Well, what *are* we going to do?" asked Zadook.

His father looked across the miles of ice and shook his head. "We'll have to think hard," he said.

With little axes the Eskimos chopped the snow into blocks and built igloos on the ice. Smoke drifted from a hole in every roof.

Splash by splash, icicle by icicle, throughout that short arctic day, the ice closed in.

All night long, as the merry dancers skipped and blazed above the frost-smoke, Waldo heard it tinkling and creaking and cracking as it ate up the open water.

And in the morning, when the orange sun peeped above the horizon, all that remained of the sea was a little black pool no bigger than your bedroom.

Waldo's head ached from bumping the ice to get a place to breathe.

*

Wuh – wuh – wuh – wuh!

A noise disturbed the arctic silence. Waldo looked all around.

The noise grew louder. *WUH – WUH – WUH – WUH – WUH!*

It was a helicopter.

Zadook and the other Eskimos came running from the igloos, rubbing their eyes with sleep.

But Waldo got a fright to see this enormous red insect dropping from the sky. With a flip of his tail he dived to safety.

He did not know that during the night Zadook's father had radioed for help.

The helicopter landed close to the little pool of water.

A lot of people jumped out.

"Brrr! It's cold!" The pilot blew on his fingers. "Where's this whale? Have we got the right place?"

"He was frightened by the helicopter," said Zadook. "He'll be back soon."

When Waldo surfaced again he found the pool surrounded by these new arrivals. As he blew a spout, flash guns sparkled on every side.

Reporters spoke into cameras and microphones. Some scribbled on little notepads. Their stories looked like this:

Scientists waved thermometers in the air and shook their heads. The sea had never frozen so early before, they said. The climate was changing.

Soldiers took sledgehammers and pickaxes and started to make the hole in the ice bigger. Waldo liked the soldiers best.

Television pictures flashed Waldo's story all round the world. From Vladivostock to Timbuktu, from the high Himalayas to the islands of the Pacific, people grew sad to hear about the young whale trapped in the ice.

More helicopters arrived.

"Vot ve need," said a fat Russian general with fourteen medals on his chest, "is an ice-breaker."

"Took the words right outta my

mouth," agreed a skinny American admiral whose uniform was also covered in medals. "Two ice-breakers."

"You send von," said the general. "And ve send von."

"And make 'em big-uns!" said the admiral.

Cameras flashed and whirred as they slapped each other on the back.

"You're very kind," said Waldo, and he splashed the water with his tail to please the onlookers.

The snow returned and drove everyone to shelter. Only two people remained in the open: a soldier still hammered away at the ice; Zadook, with his hood up, crouched by the water to keep Waldo company.

The snow ghosts came screaming past the icebergs. Roughly they buffeted the igloos, tipped over a helicopter, and pulled out the ropes holding down the orange tents.

"Push off!" said the brave soldier.

Angrily they seized him by the jacket and flung him into the sea. It was terribly cold. Waldo lifted him with his nose and set him back on the ice. Already the strong young soldier was freezing. Icicles hung from his elbows and chin.

Another snow ghost, secret and whispery, crept up behind Zadook. Waldo shouted. Just in time Zadook jumped aside. The snow ghost rushed past, hissing with anger.

"I think you should both go inside," said Waldo. "I'll be all right."

Zadook lowered his head against the blizzard and struggled to the igloo where his father was waiting.

The soldier retreated to his leaping orange tent. His trousers and jacket were stiff as boards. Comrades helped him inside and zipped the door shut.

Waldo was left alone in the arctic

night – alone with the wind and the snow and the icebergs and the wild pouncing ghosts.

Shortly before dawn the blizzard stopped. Carrying lanterns, the Eskimos and soldiers, scientists and reporters, emerged from their shelters and gathered round the pool.

Waldo was pleased to see them.

But the weather forecast was bad and they were all very anxious about the young whale. He had become a friend to everyone.

Later that morning the sky turned black. The golden sun was wiped off the horizon. For four days cloud and blizzard turned daylight into night.

The snow ghosts were everywhere, screaming and pushing, leaping out of the darkness.

It was a great battle to keep Waldo's pool from freezing over.

Huddled above radios in their tents, occasionally venturing out with floodlights and TV cameras, reporters broadcast the news that all the world was waiting to hear:

"The young whale is still alive ...

terrible blizzards ... daylight shortening ... ice growing thicker ... seven victims escape snow ghosts ... ice-breakers on their way."

On the fourth afternoon the snow stopped and the skies cleared. Igloos and tents had vanished beneath snow-drifts. Everyone helped to dig them out.

Far away in the brilliant air, two trails of smoke could be seen on the horizon. The ice-breakers had arrived.

All night long their masthead lights grew brighter, golden beneath the dancing stars.

The sun rose. Steadily the two ice-breakers crunched through the frozen sea towards Waldo. A big Russian flag flew from the mast of one. A giant

American flag fluttered from the mast of the other.

The sailors put on warm jackets and went out on deck. Lookouts hung from the crows'-nests.

When they spotted Waldo they gave a great cheer and blew the ships' whistles. Their shouts rang across the snowfields.

Waldo watched the ice-breakers come closer and closer. Their bows, hung with anchors, towered overhead. He had heard their engines twenty miles away. Now the crunch of ice and beat of propellers were deafening.

Inch by inch the sturdy ships crept nearer. The crowd on the ice drew back. There were only ten metres to go ... seven ..... three .... one.

Side by side the ice-breakers broke into Waldo's tiny circle of water.

Behind them, mile upon mile, a broad, black, ice-bobbing channel stretched through the snowfields.

It was party-time on the ice. The sailors threw ladders over the side and jumped down. Hands were shaken and backs were slapped. The Russians drank American coffee and the Americans drank Russian vodka. Everyone was happy.

Only Zadook was sad. His very best friend was leaving. With wide arms he hugged Waldo.

"Will you come back and see me?"

"Of course." Waldo dived to the seabed and brought up a fabulous shell.

He gave it to Zadook. "That's for a promise," he said.

Zadook kneeled close. "When?" he said.

"In the summer," said Waldo. "When your sore leg is better and you have a new kayak. We'll go exploring, far away into the Land of the Midnight Sun. Magic places where none of your people have sailed before."

"Oh, yes!" Zadook said. His black eyes shone.

Waldo waved a flipper to the gathered crowd. "Goodbye. Thank you! Everybody!"

He dived deep then turned and raced to the surface. High, high he sprang into the air and landed with a splash like a thousand fountains.

Cameras flashed. All the Eskimos and soldiers and sailors and reporters and scientists were splashed and jumped back laughing.

The happy young whale swam off down the winding channel.

It was a long journey. Fat seals snoozed on the icy banks. The little polar bear waved as he swam past. Dazzling icebergs rose against the sky.

Waldo began to sing. Ahead lay the edge of the ice, and far off the warm green seas of the south, where new adventures were waiting.

3

The Witch of Coconut Island

The sun stood overhead, so hot it almost fizzed on the ocean. White seabirds circled against the blue. As Waldo swam in the clear green water, tropical islands rose about him. The wind was sweet with the scents of seaweed, spice and flowers.

He had never been in the South Seas

before and turned towards one of the islands to explore. But as he drew close Waldo saw that this island was different from the others. Instead of rustling palm trees, the slopes were dotted with stumps. Red and speckled toadstools grew between. Bulging growths of fungus hung from the rocks.

Waldo swam into a bay to have a closer look. The half-covered wreck of a steamship jutted from the water.

At the head of the beach was a ramshackle hut built of boards and rags.

A short distance from the hut, high on a rock where the waves could not reach it, a giant blue egg stood in the sun.

Waldo decided he did not like this

island. He was just turning away when a figure appeared in the doorway of the hut. It was a woman, very short and enormously fat. She wore a ragged black dress which came to her knees. A broken crown was on her head and grey hair hung round her shoulders.

"Hey, you! Wait a minute!" She waved at Waldo and hurried back into the hut.

When she reappeared a big book was beneath one arm. Munching on a cake, she trotted down the sand to the water's edge.

Waldo regarded her warily. A big curly seashell hung from a string at her neck. She seemed to be surrounded by a cloud but as she came closer he saw that they were buzzing flies.

Even more surprising, a furry animal which scampered at her heels proved to be not a cat but a big rat, tail slithering in the sand. It raised a whiskery head and looked all round.

Waldo wanted to swim off as fast as his tail could carry him but he was a polite young whale and did not wish to be rude.

"Hello." The woman grinned, showing bad teeth, and took another bite of cake. "I'm called Duchess. What's your name?"

"Waldo Leander Fluke," he said reluctantly.

"How old are you?" Duchess asked. "Where do you come from? Would you like me to tell you a story?"

Waldo was surprised.

Without waiting for an answer, the old woman kneeled in the hot dry sand and set the book before her. The giant pages thumped and rustled as she found the place.

"This is a story all about a whale. Are you listening carefully?"

"One fine day," Duchess began, "a handsome young whale called Waldo came to the shore of Coconut Island."

"Coconut Island!" Waldo looked about him. "There aren't many coconuts."

"There aren't *any* coconuts," she corrected him. "I got rid of all the palm trees. It's much nicer like this. Anyway," she patted the rat and continued, "there he met a beautiful lady called Duchess. She was the ruler of the island and she read him a lovely poem."

With a fat finger Duchess followed the words in her book:

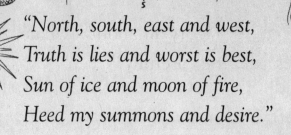

"North, south, east and west,
Truth is lies and worst is best,
Sun of ice and moon of fire,
Heed my summons and desire."

Waldo enjoyed listening to stories but this had a creepy, witchy feeling about it. The old woman read on:

"Earth, air, fire and water,
Strong is weak and long is shorter,
Spider, beetle, worm and snail,
Into a tiddler turn this whale!"

As she finished, Duchess put the twisty seashell to her lips and blew several notes like a horn:

Poo-o-o-oop! Poop-poop! Poo-o-o-oop!

Waldo did not like her story at all. As the echoes of the seashell died away he said, "I've got to go now," and lashed his tail to swim out to sea.

"You're too late! Hee-hee-hee-hee-hee!"

The old woman was right. Already a queer, tight, itchy, crinkly feeling covered him all over, from his nose to the tip of his tail. The feeling grew stronger – then stopped.

Waldo hesitated then lashed his tail again. He darted through the water. He was startled; it was so quick, so easy. He looked behind. To his astonishment his tail was right before his eyes. He was less than fifteen centimetres long! From a giant he had shrunk to the tiniest whale in the world.

Waldo lifted his head from the sea. An enormous wave – in reality little more than a ripple – washed over him. Accidentally he breathed in water. It gave him a coughing fit.

On the beach Duchess was laughing, slapping her knees and throwing her arms in the air. Like a balloon filled with jelly she shook all over.

As Waldo recovered she stood up and clapped her hands loudly. "Rokar!" she called. "Rokar! Come here, my precious. See what a treat I've got for you."

Waldo looked all round: in the air, across the waves, underwater. Who was Rokar, he wondered.

Then far away, he saw.

A gigantic eel, longer even than Waldo

when he was his proper size, came sliding through the stones and seaweed. He was dark blue and white, blotched like a leopard in the bright forest of the seabed. A fin ran the full length of his back and belly. His eyes, focused straight ahead, were wicked. His open mouth showed rows of teeth. Rokar could have bitten a whole salmon, even a small seal, in half with a single *snap*!

"Oh, help!" Waldo flipped from the waves in panic.

Rokar spotted the little splash. In the glitter of sunlight above him he saw Waldo and left the seabed like an arrow.

But although Waldo was small he was quick. As Rokar opened his mouth to strike, Waldo flipped again and sped off

in the other direction.

With a swirl of water Rokar doubled back.

Ahead of him Waldo saw the half-covered wreck. He swam towards it.

But Rokar was faster. He enjoyed the hunt and flew at Waldo a second time.

At the last split-second Waldo twisted aside. The cruel teeth snapped shut on water.

Up and down, left and right, Waldo darted and turned. Close on his tail Rokar twisted in coils and figures of eight. Again and again he struck.

Then suddenly, to his surprise, the fierce eel found himself tangled in a knot. He quickly unravelled but it gave Waldo the seconds he needed. Headlong he raced to the wrecked steamship and shot in through a porthole.

The next moment Rokar was there, his head blocking out the wavy sunlight. But Rokar was too big to squeeze through the hole. For the present, at least, Waldo was safe.

Rokar stared into the shadows. He knew ways into the wreck but there were too many iron crannies where his prey could hide. Hissing and tearing up clumps of weed in anger, he swam off.

Waldo's heart was thumping. Also, although he was so little he was still a whale and he was running short of breath. At once he set off through the half-sunken wreck, seeking a way to the surface.

He was in the engine-room, a big open space with giant boilers and shafts and walkways crossing the green shadows. Shoals of tiny fish swam in stripes of sunlight.

Waldo swam upwards and out through a blue, half-open doorway. A passage led to a flight of stairs. A human skeleton lay on the deck. Quickly Waldo swam past.

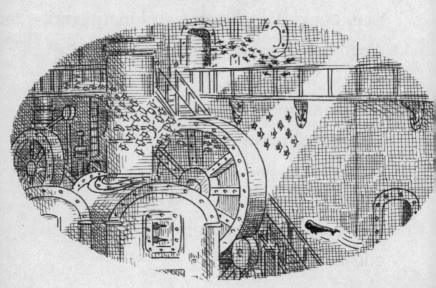

Cabins opened to right and left. He peeped into one and saw a bunk, a wardrobe, a washbasin with a mirror. A lobster had made its home in an open drawer.

Waldo hurried on and up the watery staircase. A broken door hung from one hinge. Beyond was brightness. Cautiously he swam through.

The dining saloon where Waldo now found himself was only half submerged. The surface of the sea rippled above tables. With relief Waldo blew a tiny spout and took several lungfuls of air.

He gazed around. Crystal chandeliers were hung with moss and shells. Dazzling sunbeams shone through seaweed that covered the portholes like curtains.

Everything was tilted. Goblets, plates and dining-room silver had crashed to the deck and lay heaped in sandy corners. Starfish and sea-urchins clung to chairs.

Waldo was trying to adjust to this strange world when he spotted a movement above the water, a glimpse of colour. At once he retreated beneath a table and watched.

The surface was broken. Two small feet, tipped with claws, appeared underwater, followed by a pair of scaly legs. Then with a splash and surge of bubbles, an extraordinary creature plunged into the flooded saloon.

Waldo pressed back in alarm. It was a dragon – admittedly quite a small dragon, less than sixty centimetres tall – with a tail like the end of a spear, little scaly wings, spikes down its back, and a long head ending in wide nostrils. Mostly its body was green, with a primrose belly and touches of gold and red.

"Hello." The dragon looked all round. "Where are you?"

Despite its appearance the dragon was not really frightening. Its voice was friendly.

"I saw Rokar chase you. You swam awfully well."

Waldo thought he might venture out.

"Don't be scared," said the dragon. "Look, I'll sit up here out of the water."

It climbed on to a table.

Waldo swam to a safe distance and raised his head above the ripples.

"I saw Duchess shrink you as well," the dragon continued. "With her book of spells. It makes her the most powerful witch in this part of the ocean."

"Did she shrink you too?" Waldo was startled, his voice had become high and squeaky.

"No, I'm small because I'm only seven," said the dragon, "but I'm growing bigger. What's your name?"

Waldo told him.

"I'm called Smoo," said the dragon. "My dad was the ruler of this island, the proper ruler, Alfalfa the Absolute. Until *she* came along and spoiled everything." A tear ran down his nose.

"What happened?" Waldo swam closer.

"It was a stormy day, about a year ago." Smoo rubbed his eyes with the back of a claw. "I saw this big box floating out at sea. The waves were enormous but Dad pushed the rowing-boat out and he towed the box ashore. We could hardly get it open, somebody had fastened the top down with millions of nails. Duchess was crouched up inside, wet hair all over her face. She was terrified 'cos she can't swim. I don't know where she came from but she had this sack with her, full of the remains of what she'd eaten – bits of orange peel and gnawed bones and things. And something else hidden right at the bottom."

"Her book of spells!"

"That's right," Smoo said. "Wrapped up in rags to keep it dry. She must have smuggled it past whoever nailed her in there."

"Well if she had the book, why didn't she use her magic to stop the storm and get ashore?"

"I don't know. Maybe it was too dark to see. And the box was half full of seawater – the pages would have got soaking wet."

"What happened then?"

"We helped her out," Smoo said. "Dad gave her a meal and a nice place to sleep. We were sorry for her. Next morning the storm had died down and the sun was shining. We all went down to the beach and she said she'd tell us a story out of her book."

"That's what she told me!" Waldo exclaimed.

"I know. It wasn't a story at all. First she put Dad into an egg and stood it on top of that rock so she can laugh at him and he gets baking hot in the sun."

"Your dad's in that blue egg?"

Smoo nodded. "And she took his crown." He blinked hard. "Then she made all the trees and flowers and fruit disappear, and fungus and toadstools grow everywhere. And she turned the monkeys into rats, and all the pretty birds into flies and bluebottles."

"It's horrid!" Waldo said.

"After that," Smoo said, "she tried to catch me but I swam away. So she got this eel and said a spell over him so he grew and grew."

"Rokar," Waldo said. "The opposite of what she did to me."

"And she sent him to kill me!" said Smoo. "But I hid here in the wreck of the *Albatross*."

"For a whole year?"

"They think I escaped to one of the other islands." Smoo drew back the weed at a porthole and pointed. "I don't know how, 'cos she smashed the rowing-boat. Maybe she thinks I can fly. Anyway, they've stopped searching."

"What do you eat?" Waldo asked.

"Seaweed and winkles." Smoo made a face. "They're not very nice."

"So now Duchess is the ruler of Coconut Island," Waldo said.

"More like Fungus Island," Smoo said gloomily. "Everybody hates her, all the dolphins and visiting birds and everybody. But they're frightened of her – and Rokar. There's nothing they can do."

Waldo looked round the flooded saloon. "What happened to the sailors off the ship?"

"The survivors made a raft and sailed away," Smoo said. "It was ages ago, before I was born."

The tide was coming in and soon the *Albatross* was completely under water.

Smoo took Waldo a guided tour of the ship. They swam from the bottom of the hold – where Waldo was introduced to the resident crabs and catfish – to the bridge with its wheel and engine controls, and even inside the black and orange funnel.

*

The sun sank into the ocean. The sky was spangled with tropical stars.

Smoo, who could breathe water *and* air, had a comfortable bed in the captain's cabin. Waldo drifted, sinking down through the ship and rising again as the tide came in.

All night he racked his brains. *What* could he do to break Duchess's spells – particularly the one that had made him so small. He was a whale! He couldn't stay the size of a tiddler for the rest of his life.

The sky was turning pink with dawn when at last Waldo had the beginnings of an idea. He thought about it very hard.

After a seaweed breakfast he told his

plan to Smoo. "Do you think it will work?" he asked anxiously.

"It might," Smoo said. "But be careful she doesn't put another spell on you."

"And Rokar doesn't slide up when I'm not looking!" Waldo shivered.

"I'll keep a special lookout," Smoo assured him.

Nervously Waldo swam from the doorway of the bridge. The sea glittered.

"Hey! Duchess!" He shouted to be heard above the softly-breaking waves. "Come here a minute. I want to ask you something."

In her patched hut at the head of the beach Duchess heard his squeak. Her grinning head appeared in the doorway.

"Rokar not got you yet?" She sniggered. "He must be saving you for lunch."

"He didn't catch me yesterday."

"He will today."

"You're really not a very *good* witch are you?" Waldo tried to keep his voice from shaking. He was terrified.

"WHAT!" Duchess rushed down the beach to the water's edge. "What did you say?"

The flies boiled round her.

"Getting a slimy beast like Rokar to do half your work. Can't do any magic at all without your shell and your book of spells."

"Who can't!" screeched Duchess. "I can do anything I want!"

"Go on then." Waldo pointed to a

sea-ringed rock at the mouth of the bay. "Make an orange tree grow on that rock if you're so clever."

"I don't want to!" snapped Duchess.

"See," Waldo mocked. "You can't."

Duchess hopped with rage. "Just you wait!" She ran back up the beach and returned clutching her enormous book.

Three rats accompanied her, gambolling round her feet. She tripped on one and nearly fell. Angrily she kicked them out of the way.

"I'm not staying here," Waldo shouted. "You'll put another spell on me."

"No I won't. What did you want? An orange tree? On that rock there?"

She fell to her knees in the dry sand and threw over the pages.

"Ah!" She found the place. "I'll show you!" She pushed back her hair and pointed at the foam-fringed rock.

Waldo was too far off to hear her words but the notes of the seashell reached him clearly:

Poo-o-o-o-o-oop! *Poo-o-o-o-o-oop!*
Poop!

Duchess threw wide her arms.

Waldo looked towards the rock. A thin twig had appeared on top. Quickly it grew – a metre, two metres, five metres – and put out branches. Seconds later it was hung with dazzling oranges.

Waldo was impressed. Although Duchess was horrible, he clapped his flippers.

"See!" She turned boastfully. "I can do anything. Why don't you swim across and taste one – half are poisoned!" She cackled. "What else? Go on, ask me another."

"No, you might spell me," Waldo said again. "Or get Rokar to creep round and gobble me up."

"I told you, I won't." Duchess was

longing to show off. "What would you like – an elephant? Thunder and lightning?"

Waldo looked up at the blue, baking-hot sky. "A blizzard of snow," he said. "A heavy rainstorm with no clouds."

She glanced at her book of spells. "No, the pages would get wet. Not rain or snow. But I could."

"All right," Waldo said, "then turn all your flies into butterflies."

"Butterflies! Ugh! But if that's what you want."

Again Duchess rustled the pages of her book, chanted her spell and blew the horn:

Poop! Poop-poop! Poop-poop-poop!

The next moment the flies which buzzed all around her had changed into a cloud of beautiful butterflies. The bluebottles on the fungus became ten thousand more.

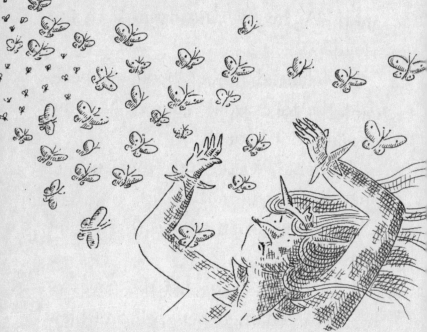

"Aah! Aah!" Duchess covered her head with her arms and stumbled away. "Disgusting! Disgusting!"

The cloud cleared and she looked across the water at Waldo. "I told you, I can do anything."

The butterflies, finding Coconut Island not to their liking, flew off to another island, a dancing procession across the sea.

Waldo watched them go. "I agree you can do lots of things – but not *anything*."

"What can't I do?" Duchess stamped her foot. "Go on, tell me."

"Am I still safe?"

"Yes, yes."

Waldo swam round the anchor and pointed to the big blue egg on its high rock. "Make that egg hatch out."

"Oh, that's too easy." Duchess crossed the sand and clambered up. "I could let you out any time, couldn't I?" She tapped the shell with her knuckles. "Are you nice and scrunched up in there? It's going to be a really *hot* day."

The egg shook. From within there was a sound of angry shouting.

Duchess giggled. "Don't run away." She climbed back down. "No, not the egg, that's special."

"Not water," Waldo said, "not the egg. You're very choosy."

"Anything else," she said. "Something harder."

Waldo took a deep breath. "All right." It was the moment he had been waiting for. "Even a witch as strong as you can't control the tide."

"The tide? Of course I can."

"Make the sea come in and go out?"

"I do it all the time."

"Not without your book."

"I said I can do it!" she repeated crossly.

"I don't believe you," Waldo said. "Prove it. Make the tide go out now."

"Is that all you want?"

"Right out past the *Albatross*." He pointed.

"To the mouth of the bay?"

"That rock with the orange tree on it."

"Easy."

"Then walk out without getting your feet wet and pick one."

She paused. "If I pick one will you eat it?"

"I'm a whale," Waldo said. "I don't eat oranges. Besides, an orange is as big as me now. And you might pick a poisoned one."

"No I won't." Duchess wobbled with merriment. "I'll pick one if you promise to eat a bit."

Waldo thought. "All right. I don't believe you can do it anyway. But if you walk out and pick an orange, I'll eat a big mouthful."

Duchess bustled up the beach to her book of spells and kneeled in the sand. "Tide out," she muttered happily, "tide out," and ran her finger down the index. "Ah, there it is!" She threw over the heavy pages.

The sun was hot. She scratched her wild hair and jammed the crown back on. Then sitting on her heels, Duchess looked towards the lapping waves and chanted her spell. Again Waldo could not make out the words but the notes of the twisty shell rang clearly across the bay:

Poop-poop! Poo-o-o-o-oop! Poop-poop!

As the spell was finished, the crystal water began to suck and slide back down the sand, tugging pebbles and weed in its wake. Waldo felt himself being swept away by the current and just managed to swim to the safety of the *Albatross*. With all his strength he dived through the emptying dining-saloon and passages into the engine-room.

Back and back retreated the water, surging over rocks, leaving the great steamship exposed to its keel and giant propeller. Coral and clams that had never felt the brush of the wind and bite of the sun were laid bare. Bright fish spilled in waterfalls from the portholes of the *Albatross*. Rokar, creeping up despite Duchess's promise, was stranded on the seaweed, white blotches on midnight blue and as long as a cricket pitch. Quickly he wriggled back into the ebbing sea.

In minutes the magic was complete. The sand settled. All round the bay the ocean stood upright in a wall of water ten metres high. Blue-green, like an aquarium with no glass, it shimmered and wobbled in the sun.

Smoo, who all the time had been peeping from the bridge of the ship, ran through dripping corridors and scrambled down ladders to join Waldo.

Only a pool remained in the bottom of the *Albatross*. Side by side the two friends watched Duchess through a porthole.

Right and left she gazed across the bay, for in the swirl of retreating water the little figure of Waldo had disappeared.

"Where are you?" Leaving her book of spells, she walked down the beach. Already the hard wet sand was steaming in the sun.

Smoo ducked from sight.

"I'm here." Waldo called from the shadow of the toppled ship.

She spotted his face at the porthole. "You said I couldn't do it!" she crowed. "Now I'm going to walk out to the tree and pick an orange."

"A nice sweet one," Waldo said.

"Of course! Hee-hee-hee-hee!" She hurried on, skipping round rocks and jumping over trickles that ran down the sand.

"She's gone," Waldo said.

Smoo rejoined him at the porthole.

Together they watched the witch's retreating back then looked up the beach. Forgotten but safe – as Duchess thought – her book of spells lay open in the dry sand.

"Are you ready?" Waldo said.

Smoo shivered. "I think so."

"All her power *is* in the book of spells, isn't it?"

"And the shell, yes."

"What does the shell *do*?" Waldo asked.

"I think it makes the spell work," Smoo replied. "She says the words then blows the shell and that sort of switches the magic on."

Waldo thought about it. "Anyway, she doesn't want the book to get wet," he said, "not even rained on."

A snatch of song reached them on the wind. Duchess was singing.

Nervously Smoo eased his little wings and stretched his claws. "I'll go now," he said.

"Good luck," Waldo said. "Watch out for Rokar."

The porthole was too high for Smoo to jump to the sand. Quickly he ran through the ship and climbed down the rusty anchor chain. Then, hiding behind the *Albatross*, creeping through pools and dashing from stone to stone, he made his way up the seashore. At one point the only hiding place was right beside the swaying wall of water. Coloured fish swam high above his head. Rokar watched from the watery depths.

Smoo reached the side of the beach. Panting, he lay on his belly and peeped through the withered grasses. A short distance away the book of spells lay on the bright sand. Far down the bay Duchess skipped towards the orange tree, her black rags fluttering in the breeze.

Smoo drew a deep breath. Greatly frightened, he emerged from hiding and tiptoed across the beach.

Suddenly a loud cry rang out: "Mistress! Mistress!"

Smoo froze. He looked all round.

It was the book of spells. It had a voice. It was shouting: "Come back! There's an intruder! Hurry!"

Duchess had almost reached the orange tree. She spun round. Through wisps of steam she saw the little dragon. "Smoo! I thought you..."

But already the brave Smoo was racing forward. The book lay before him, ancient pages covered with writing. It was too big for him to carry. With one claw he grabbed a cover and ran off, trailing the book behind.

"Help!" the book yelled. "Help! Mistress! He's heading for the water!"

Duchess screamed. Leaving the

orange tree and cliff-high wall of water, she raced back up the shore.

"Thief!" she shrieked. "Villain! I'll turn you into a worm! A shrimp!" Her broken crown tumbled to the sand. She left it where it lay. "Stop!"

But Smoo didn't stop. Desperation gave him strength. Across the beach he struggled, over the stones and spiky grass, up through banks of toadstools.

A big rat, higher than his knees, jumped out at him, squeaking and biting. Smoo dropped the book and gave the rat a scratch. It ran away.

Far behind but catching up at every stride, Duchess ran across the hard sand. Her grey hair flew, her bare feet splashed in the puddles. She passed the *Albatross* and soon was scrambling up the sliding sand of the beach.

The hillside grew steeper. Smoo heaved the book through stones and smelly fungus.

"Wait!" Duchess clawed her way up the slope. "Stop now and I'll forgive you!"

Smoo reached his destination, a flat rock high above the sea.

"No, master!" the book pleaded. "Not the sea! Ple-e-ease! Not the water!"

Smoo hesitated. Then he thought of all the evil the book had brought: his father, the island, Rokar, Waldo, and much much more. Duchess was almost upon him. With both arms he flung the fluttering book as far out into the sea as his strength could manage.

"Aaahhh!" screamed the book as it fell.

"Aaahhh!" shrieked Duchess as she saw it go.

"Aaahhh!" yelled Smoo as Duchess ran at him and sent him tumbling head over tail into the water.

Chaos was let loose upon Coconut Island!

As the book sank into the green sea the ink dissolved from its pages. And as each page washed blank, the spell written upon it was broken.

The first, by chance, was the very last to be made. With a tremendous roar the towering walls of water collapsed. White and foaming, the ocean crashed up the bay and right across the island, carrying everything in its path. The *Albatross* was swept high up the beach. Duchess's hut was smashed to splinters. The blue egg was carried far out to sea.

And while everything was still confusion, water streaming from the highest rocks, Coconut Island returned to its previous state. The dead stumps of palm trees grew golden and tall; feathery branches nodded against the sky. Toadstools were transformed into tropical flowers. Ugly humps of fungus became fragrant herbs. Cool lemon groves grew above the beach.

And in the sea, scores of rats which had been swept away by the tidal wave, changed back into monkeys. All round the island the bright water was dotted with heads as they swam ashore.

Waldo, by the greatest of good luck, was washed from a porthole of the *Albatross*; had he returned to his proper size inside the ship, he would have been trapped and cramped up for life. Briefly, still the size of a tiddler, he lay flipping and jumping on the beach, then streams of returning water carried him back into the sea.

To his horror, as the water cleared, there was Rokar, hunting the rocks and weed for prey.

Waldo darted between two stones. Rokar had not seen him. Then the last of the inky spell that had shrunk Waldo rinsed from the page and he felt himself growing bigger. The stones where he was hiding rolled aside. In seconds he was the size of a dolphin.

Now Rokar did see him. Like a spear he flew at Waldo, jaws gaping to deliver a wicked bite. Waldo fled out to sea. Rokar doubled back and chased after him. His mouth opened to bite off Waldo's tail. But Waldo was growing all the time and now he was faster. He shot ahead. Rokar was left behind.

Soon Waldo was again his normal size. What a relief! He took a deep breath and blew a high sparkling spout.

A mile distant the palm trees of Coconut Island rose above the golden sand. Waldo was safe, he had escaped. But what about brave Smoo? And the terrifying Rokar, even now much longer than himself? And evil Duchess without her book of spells? And Smoo's dad, still trapped in the blue egg?

Waldo sprang into the air and landed with a terrific *splash*! Then, ready to fight a battle for his friend, he headed back to the island.

Rokar was there, a coiling shape in the distance. Waldo swam to meet him.

With a thump and boil of water that turned the sea to foam, they clashed and struggled. Rokar's sharp teeth cut Waldo's side, his long body wrapped round and round him. But suddenly, with a twist, Waldo had Rokar at his mercy. He opened his mouth to give him a bite that would rid Coconut Island once and for all of the giant eel.

But Rokar was lucky. At that very moment, hundreds of metres away in the sea, several pages of Duchess's book which had stuck together floated apart, and the spell which had made Rokar so big was washed away.

To Waldo's astonishment the wicked head and thick neck disappeared, the tight coils slithered from his body. He looked right and left. Rokar appeared to have vanished. Then he saw a little spotted eel, no longer than the span of your fingers. It was Rokar. Squeaking with fright he swam down to the seabed and hid beneath trailing weed.

A crab snapped at him with sharp claws. With a shriek Rokar darted out. Where could he go? Everybody hated him now.

"It serves you right!" Waldo left him to his fate and swam away.

The steamship *Albatross* lay at the head of the beach, well above high water and almost on an even keel.

The little figure of Smoo stood high on the bridge. Waldo waved. Smoo was shouting – but another voice was in Waldo's ears. It was Duchess.

"Help!" she was screaming. "Help! I can't swim!"

The great wave and the tide had combined to form a whirlpool. Round and round it foamed off the rocky point of the island. Duchess had been caught by the spinning current. Grey hair trailing, she drew closer and closer to the vortex.

"He-e-e-elp!"

Waldo raced towards her shouts and was just in time to catch the fat old witch as she was sucked down through the whirling bubbles. A few sweeps of his tail carried them to safety.

With sharp teeth he snipped through the string round Duchess's neck and watched her magic shell drift down to join a thousand non-magic shells on the seabed. A crab scuttled to investigate. A thin cloud of sand settled upon the twisty shell. It was gone.

Holding Duchess by the back of her dress, Waldo carried her to the sea-ringed rock from which the orange tree had now disappeared.

"The sun will soon dry you." He floated away. "No book of spells; no magic shell; you can't swim. I think you'll be safe there for a while."

"Curse you, whale!" Not the least grateful for her rescue, Duchess spat at him and threw stones.

Waldo ignored her for Smoo was still shouting from the bridge of the *Albatross*. He strained to hear.

"My dad!" The little dragon was pointing. "The egg! The sea's carrying him away!"

For unnoticed by anyone, as Smoo

flung the book of spells into the ocean, a single page had torn free and blown back on to the island. Now it was caught in the branches of a pomegranate tree. On this page was the spell that had imprisoned Smoo's father, Alfalfa the Absolute, inside the blue egg.

Now, far off and barely visible even from Smoo's high position, he was drifting away to be lost for ever – or possibly eaten by some enormous fish.

Waldo set off in the direction Smoo was pointing. Coconut Island was soon far behind him – but where was the egg? He leaped high into the air and looked all round. At once he saw it, quite close at hand, blue as the sky and bobbing in the green waves. Waldo swam across and took it gently in his jaws.

"Oh my goodness!" A peppery voice came from inside the egg. "What's happening now?"

Waldo let go for a moment. "You're quite safe," he said. "I'm a friend of Smoo. We've taken the witch prisoner. I'm carrying you back to the island. We'll soon have you out of there."

Smoo stood on the beach. With a smooth stone he hammered at the egg which contained his father.

"Go on, give it a clout!" exclaimed Alfalfa irritably. "Hurry up! You're giving me a terrible headache."

"I am trying, Dad!" said Smoo. "But the shell's so thick." He whacked the egg again.

"Would you like me to try?" Waldo watched from the shallows. The tropical waves splashed over his back.

Smoo bowled the big blue egg to the shore and floated it out. "You will be careful," he said anxiously.

Waldo took the egg in his back teeth like a nut and bit hard. Smoo was right, the shell was very strong. He screwed up his face and *crunched*.

With a bang like a gun going off the blue egg broke open.

"Oh help! What next!" exclaimed the dishevelled ruler of Coconut Island as he looked around and found himself in a big pink mouth with strong white teeth.

Mixed with bits of eggshell he tumbled into the water.

Alfalfa the Absolute, despite his title, was quite a small dragon. But he was kind and much loved. The moment he appeared, all the monkeys came scampering from high branches and sunny cliffs. And all the birds, which first had been turned into flies, then butterflies, came swooping back across the ocean.

Reaching the beach, Alfalfa hugged his son and clapped the battered crown, which Smoo had recovered from a rock pool, upon his head.

"I have three royal pronouncements to make," Alfalfa declared grandly.

"First: the wicked witch Duchess shall be banished for seven years to the tiny Isle of Stones where nothing grows and the sea-current is strong. She shall live in the cave and eat whatever weed the sea washes up.

"Second: we shall make the good ship *Albatross* our palace. We shall wash out the sand, paint it and polish it, and all good creatures who visit Coconut Island will be made welcome.

"And third," Alfalfa waded out to Waldo and tapped him on the shoulders with a stalk of seaweed. "Your title henceforward is *Waldo the Mighty*, and we invest you with the decoration of CWE First Class."

"Thank you very much," Waldo said shyly. "What's CWE?"

"Conqueror of Witches and Eels," said Alfalfa.

Waldo splashed his tail with pleasure. The bright drops sparkled like a rainbow in the sunshine.

The End